FROGGY RIDES A BIKE

FROGGY RIDES
A BIKE

by JONATHAN LONDON
illustrated by FRANK REMKIEWICZ

SCHOLASTIC INC.
New York Toronto London Auckland Sydney
Mexico City New Delhi Hong Kong Buenos Aires

For Spencer and Macy, who inspired this story,
and for Sean, Aaron, Natalia, Abby, and Shai—who did, too
        —J.L.

For the children of New Orleans
        —F.R.

ISBN-13: 978-0-545-03808-9
ISBN-10: 0-545-03808-1

Text copyright © 2006 by Jonathan London.
Illustrations copyright © 2006 by Frank Remkiewicz.
All rights reserved. Published by Scholastic Inc., 557 Broadway, New York, NY 10012,
by arrangement with Viking, a division of Penguin Young Readers Group, a member of
Penguin Group (USA) Inc. SCHOLASTIC and associated logos are trademarks and/or
registered trademarks of Scholastic Inc.

12 11 10 9 8 7 6 5 4 3 2 1   7 8 9 10 11/0

Printed in the U.S.A.   40
First Scholastic paperback printing, September 2007

Set in Kabel

Froggy looked out the window.
His shiny new bike gleamed in the sun.
"Yippee!" he said . . .

and he flopped outside
and hopped on his bike—*flop flop . . . bing!*—
and took off.

He pedaled so fast
that soon he was going about
a million miles an hour!

He pedaled so fast
that soon he was flying
high in the sky—

WHEEEEE!

And there was his dad
far, far below, calling,

FRROOGGYY!

Froggy stopped
flying.

He was falling . . .

falling . . .

He woke up and rubbed his eyes.
"Rise and shine, Froggy!" said his dad.
"Today's the day we get your bike!"

"Yippee!" cried Froggy.
He bounced out of bed and flopped
into the kitchen—*flop flop flop!*

"Let's go," said Froggy.
"Okay," said his dad.
"But first you have to get dressed!"
"Oops!" said Froggy.

And he flopped back
to his bedroom
to get dressed—
*zip! zoop! zup!
zut! zut! zut!*

At the bike shop,
Froggy said, "I want a *trick* bike!"
"But, Froggy," said his dad,
"first you have to learn
how to ride a bike!"

"Okay," said Froggy.
"But I get to pick
it out! That one!"
"Too big," said Dad.

"That one!"
"Too expensive," said Dad.

"*That* one!" said Froggy.
"It's the bike of my dreams!"

"Okey-doke!" said Dad.
"Yippee!" cried Froggy.
"My very first bike!
But now I need a horn and a bell!"
"Both?" said Dad. "Okey-doke!"
And Froggy got a horn and a bell—
honk honk! ting-a-ling!

Back at home,
everybody gathered around to watch.
All of Froggy's friends were there—
even Frogilina.
"Okay, Froggy," said his dad.
"Now hop on and pedal like mad.
I won't let go!"

"Okay," said Froggy.
"But first you have to put my horn on. And my bell.
Then I'll ride my bike!"

Froggy's dad put his horn on—*honk honk!*
"Now hop on and pedal like mad," he said.
"I won't let go."
"Okay," said Froggy.
"But you still have to put my bell on.
Then I'll ride my bike!"

Froggy's dad put his bell on—*ting-a-ling!*
"Now hop on and pedal like mad," he said.
"I won't let go."

So Froggy hopped on his bike—*flop flop . . . bing!*—
and pedaled like mad—*honk honk! ting-a-ling!*
zoom zoom zoom!
But then Froggy's dad . . .

"Yikes!" cried Froggy.
His bike zigged and zagged and wobbled.
He was falling . . . falling . . .

Thump! He fell on his bottom.
Frogilina giggled.

Froggy's dad helped him up
and said, "Good job, Froggy!
Now hop on again and pedal like mad!
I won't let go!"

Froggy rubbed his bottom
and hopped on his bike—*flop flop . . . bing!*—
and pedaled like mad—*honk honk! ting-a-ling!*
zoom zoom zoom!
But Froggy's dad . . .
let go again!
Froggy's friends shouted, "Go, Froggy, go!"

"Yikes!" cried Froggy.
His bike zigged and zagged and wobbled.
He was falling . . . falling . . .

But in the morning,
Froggy hopped on his bike—*flop flop . . . bing!*
honk honk! ting-a-ling! zoom zoom zoom—
and popped wheelies . . .

all day long—*boing! boing! boing!*